For Fred's grandchildren,
Isabella & Alfredo Marcellino

For Judy & April—E.P.

A
atheneum

ATHENEUM BOOKS FOR YOUNG READERS • An imprint of Simon & Schuster Children's Publishing Division • 1230 Avenue of the Americas, New York, New York 10020 • Copyright © 2019 by The Estate of Fred Marcellino • All rights reserved, including the right of reproduction in whole or in part in any form. • ATHENEUM BOOKS FOR YOUNG READERS is a registered trademark of Simon & Schuster, Inc. • Atheneum logo is a trademark of Simon & Schuster, Inc. • For information about special discounts for bulk purchases, please contact Simon & Schuster Special Sales at 1-866-506-1949 or business@simonandschuster.com. • The Simon & Schuster Speakers Bureau can bring authors to your live event. For more information or to book an event, contact the Simon & Schuster Speakers Bureau at 1-866-248-3049 or visit our website at www.simonspeakers.com. • Book design by Fred Marcellino • The text for this book was set in Bernhard Modern. • The illustrations for this book were rendered in watercolor. • Manufactured in China • 0619 SCP • First Edition • 10 9 8 7 6 5 4 3 2 1 • CIP data for this book is available from the Library of Congress. • ISBN 978-1-5344-0401-4 • ISBN 978-1-5344-0402-1 (eBook) • Ages 4–8 • 0919

ARRIVEDERCI, CROCODILE or SEE YOU LATER ALLIGATOR

WANTED

REWARD

begun by FRED MARCELLINO

and completed by ERIC PUYBARET

A CAITLYN DLOUHY BOOK • ATHENEUM BOOKS FOR YOUNG READERS

New York London Toronto Sydney New Delhi

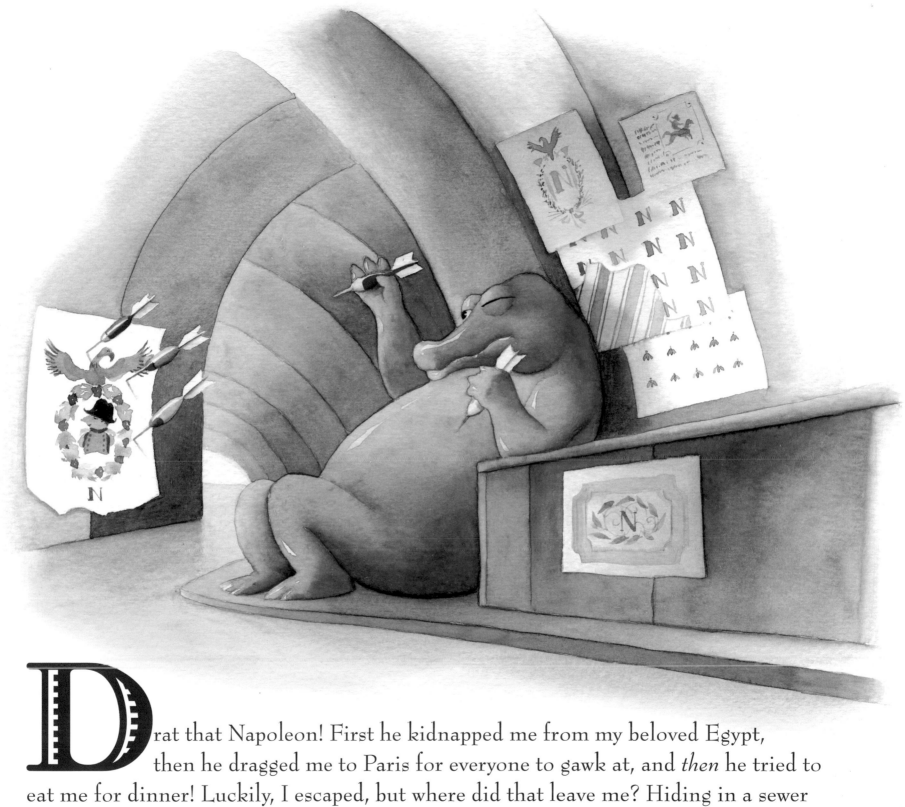

Drat that Napoleon! First he kidnapped me from my beloved Egypt, then he dragged me to Paris for everyone to gawk at, and *then* he tried to eat me for dinner! Luckily, I escaped, but where did that leave me? Hiding in a sewer with nothing to eat.

And I mean *nothing*. No pelicans, no flamingos—not even a frog. I was wasting away—a shadow of my former self. I even had a few cavities. Oh, to get out of that town!

Then one day a newspaper headline caught my eye—

NAPOLEON TO TOUR ITALY: FIRST STOP, VENICE

Venice? Perfect! A watery city of canals and Italian food. What more could a crocodile want? Cannelloni, here I come!

I slithered out early the next morning and found a hiding place in Napoleon's caravan. The trip? *Very* tedious (see below).

PARIS

VENICE

TRAVEL RATING

LODGING *don't ask*

FOOD *self-service*

SERVICE *none*

Finally, we reached the coast and hopped a royal barge. Destination: VENICE.

Well, if Paris
was all useless parks and grand
boulevards, Venice was just the opposite—
convenient canals for swimming around town,
and lots of open squares with food for sale. I couldn't
begin to identify all the goodies on display.

And, atop a large column,
a statue of—yes—a crocodile!
This was more like it. A town
where food *and* crocodiles
were appreciated!

As usual, that vandal Napoleon had his eye on everything. Treasures flowed out of palaces, to be crated for shipment back to Paris.

"Get me paintings," he screamed, "lots of them! Sculptures, too! And tapestries, silver, gold. You name it—I want it!"

Boy, would I love to teach that bully a lesson in manners! But for the moment, I opted for a swim and a bite to eat.

Getting around the canals was so easy. This town was made for a crocodile!

I was about to check out the local market when suddenly I was distracted by the most heavenly aroma.

Nearby, at an outdoor cafe, a customer was being served a heaping bowl of pasta with *ragù alla* Bolognese. I was so enchanted that I thoughtlessly wandered out into the sunlight to get a better whiff.

In a flash I was surrounded by
a band of costumed revelers.
   "Superb," one shouted.
   "How original!" cried another.
"A dragon."
   "Oh, don't be silly," a third
person snapped. "He's supposed
to be a crocodile. Right?"
   All I could do was nod.
   "It's the best costume
ever!" they all cried.
"Come join us for lunch."

What charming company.
And what a delicious meal!
Spaghetti with meatballs, veal
scaloppine, and eggplant parmigiana,
followed by mixed greens,
Gorgonzola cheese, and crusty
bread. I skipped the cappuccino.
No one could stop talking
about the new guest.
    "Extraordinary outfit!" said one.
    "Do you believe those teeth?"
said another.
    "And that appetite!
Very crocodile."

I had a few bowls of gelato and
a cheesecake to top things off.
I could tell my new friends
were impressed.

"Ciao, *coccodrillo*," they all cried.
"You must come to the grand
ball tonight."

Costume ball? Oh, I don't know. Then again,
don't they always serve suckling pigs or
pheasants at these fancy dos?

Maybe I'd give it a try.
But first things first.
Nap time!

When I awoke, starving, it was already dusk, and the streets were filled with laughing partygoers. Following the crowd, I found myself at the brightly lit palazzo.

What a splendid affair! And I fit in so effortlessly. Everyone was enchanted by my "outfit."

"Just like the crocodile statue in the piazza," someone said.

"Fabulous workmanship," gushed another. "I bet the costume was made in Milan."

Flattering, yes . . . but I couldn't keep my eyes off the buffet table!

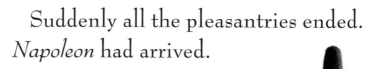

Suddenly all the pleasantries ended.
Napoleon had arrived.

I slid behind a column.
Rats! Would I be recognized?

Luckily, at that moment the orchestra struck up a
lively tune, and everyone headed for the dance floor.
This was my chance to duck for cover—and maybe grab
a snack or two on the way out.

But now what? A rather forward young lady
was whisking me off for a dance.
    I briefly struggled to get away but—
oh, that music—a catchy mazurka!
Who could resist?
    Not this crocodile.

Sure, the steps were new, but when you've got crocodile rhythm and grace, you catch on fast. My partner was a natural too — but could she handle some *Egyptian* dances?

I started with an old standard,
the rather staid Mummy Minuet.
Easy enough.

Then, for a change of pace,
a lively Palm-Palm. Boy,
she caught on fast.

Then the King Tut Strut,

the Egyptian Conniption . . .

Then a hush came over the room as Napoleon strode across the floor. Thrusting an accusing arm at me, he hissed, "I'd know that crocodile anywhere! He's mine! I was supposed to have him for dinner!"

Everyone stared in disbelief at this rude intruder.

My lovely young partner
stepped forward.

"You go too far, sir!" she said.
"It's one thing stealing paintings
and tapestries, but quite another
to insult the star of the ball."

A roar of approval arose from
the crowd.

They hoisted me on their shoulders,
and we made a dash for the piazza.
What fun to see the sputtering Napoleon
and his crew chasing after us.
"Arrest that crocodile!" he screamed.
"Arrest everybody!"

Napoleon reached the waterside
too late, lost his footing, and landed in
the water. Another cheer came
from the crowd.

Well, everything should have been perfect—gondolas, moonlight, music, and merriment—but I couldn't stop thinking about that fabulous wasted buffet!

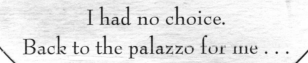

I had no choice.
Back to the palazzo for me . . .

With a little stop on the way.

From Start to Finish

Fred Marcellino was in the process of creating *Arrivederci, Crocodile*, a sequel to his gorgeously acclaimed *I, Crocodile*, when he died. He had completed the text, page layouts, and half of the finished illustrations. When Simon & Schuster acquired the rights to move toward the book's completion, they began a search for just the right illustrator, someone with a compatible vision and style, who would be able to bring their own personality to an entirely new set of illustrations while honoring Fred's intentions. It was immediately recognized by all concerned that Eric Puybaret was that exact person. To everyone's delight, it was discovered that Eric was already a great admirer of Fred's picture books—he'd discovered Fred's *Puss in Boots* years earlier in his French publisher's office, and the image of that cat had been imprinted in his mind since the early days of his career. He happily agreed to take on *Arrivederci*, and did so with diligent attention to every detail, following through with Fred's vision. The result is a collaboration in the most perfect sense—of aesthetic, of talent, of bemused adoration of one irascible crocodile.

Ciao, Crocodile, indeed.

◆

Fred Marcellino was a renowned and universally beloved artist and illustrator. After spending a year in Venice as a Fulbright Scholar, he designed record album covers for the likes of Fleetwood Mac before changing the face of book design with his elegant touch and groundbreaking vision. When he turned his attention toward children's book illustration, he won a Caldecott Honor for his first full-color picture book, *Puss in Boots*, and went on to redefine such classics as *The Steadfast Tin Soldier* and *The Pelican Chorus*. His first book as author and illustrator, *I, Crocodile*, was proclaimed a "pièce de résistance" by *Publishers Weekly* and was a *New York Times* Best Book of the Year.

Eric Puybaret's fine artwork is displayed at Galerie Robillard in Paris, and he has illustrated a number of equally exquisite children's books, including *Suite for Human Nature*; the bestselling *Puff, the Magic Dragon*; and *The Night Before Christmas*; as well as many others in his native country, France. His paintings have been praised by the *New York Times* as "elegantly rendered" and *Kirkus Reviews* has called them "dreamlike." More can be seen at EricPuybaret.com.